The Princess and the Frog

By Margaret Nash
Illustrated by Martin Remphry

Special thanks to our advisers for their expertise:

Adria F. Klein, Ph.D.
Professor Emeritus, California State University
San Bernardino, California

Susan Kesselring, M.A.
Literacy Educator
Rosemount-Apple Valley-Eagan (Minnesota) School District

PICTURE WINDOW BOOKS
Minneapolis, Minnesota

Levels for *Read-it!* Readers

- Familiar topics
- Frequently used words
- Repeating patterns

- New ideas
- Larger vocabulary
- Variety of language structures

- Challenges in ideas
- Expanded vocabulary
- Wide variety of sentences

- More complex ideas
- Extended vocabulary range
- Expanded language structures

A Note to Parents and Caregivers:

Read-it! Readers are for children who are just starting on the amazing road to reading. These beautiful books support both the acquisition of reading skills and the love of books.

The RED LEVEL presents familiar topics using common words and repeating sentence patterns.

The BLUE LEVEL presents new ideas using a larger vocabulary and varied sentence structure.

The YELLOW LEVEL presents more challenging ideas, a broad vocabulary, and wide variety in sentence structure.

The GREEN LEVEL presents more complex ideas, an extended vocabulary range, and expanded language structures.

When sharing a book with your child, read in short stretches, pausing often to talk about the pictures. Have your child turn the pages and point to the pictures and familiar words. And be sure to reread favorite stories or parts of stories.

There is no right or wrong way to share books with children. Find time to read with your child, and pass on the legacy of literacy.

Adria F. Klein, Ph.D.
Professor Emeritus
California State University
San Bernardino, California

First American edition published in 2005 by
Picture Window Books
5115 Excelsior Boulevard
Suite 232
Minneapolis, MN 55416
877-845-8392
www.picturewindowbooks.com

First published in Great Britain by Franklin Watts, 96 Leonard Street,
London, EC2A 4XD

Printed in the United States of America.

Library of Congress Cataloging-in-Publication Data
Nash, Margaret, 1939-
The princess and the frog / by Margaret Nash ; illustrated by Martin Remphry.
p. cm. — (Read-it! readers)
Summary: When this princess kisses a frog, she lives happily ever after in a slightly different way.
ISBN 1-4048-0562-1 (hardcover)
[1. Fairy tales. 2. Princesses—Fiction. 3. Frogs—Fiction.] I. Remphry, Martin, ill. II. Title. III. Series.
PZ8.N1275Pr 2004
[E]—dc22 2004007621

Once upon a time, there was
a princess who didn't behave
like a princess.

She didn't sit on velvet cushions.

She wouldn't wear her crown.

The king didn’t know what to do with her.

"You are always jumping around," he said. "No prince will want to marry you!"

"I don't want to marry a boring old prince," said the princess.

The princess threw her golden ball. "OUT!" shouted the king, pointing at the door.

The princess took her ball to the far end of the garden and bounced it up and down. Suddenly, the ball went too far. It landed in the pond.

“OH NO!” cried the princess. She lay down at the edge of the pond and tried to reach the ball.

"Come here, ball!" she yelled, but the ball was sinking. She thought she would never see it again.

“If I get your ball, will you play with me?” The princess looked up and saw a frog sitting on a lily pad.

"Certainly," said the princess. The frog hopped off the lily pad and swam away.

The frog soon came back
with the ball in his mouth.
“Thank you,” said
the princess, and
she bowed
to him.

They played hopscotch on the path. “This is fun,” said the princess, “but now I’ve got to go back to the palace for tea.”

“Please let me come,” said the frog. The princess bent down. “OK,” she agreed, “hop on my shoulder.”

When the king opened the door,
he threw his hands up in horror.
"Look at your dirty dress!" he said.

“And WHO is that?” he asked,
pointing at her shoulder.
“CROAK!” croaked the frog.

“He’s staying for tea,” said the princess. “He found my ball, and I promised to play with him.”

"Hmmm ... ," said the king. "Well, a promise is a promise, I suppose."

The frog jumped onto the table, and the princess fed him some cake. “His table manners are terrible!” said the king.

After tea, the frog asked, “May I take a nap in your room, princess?”

“Tell him no!” said the king.

But the princess picked up the frog and carried him to her bedroom.

She put him in the sink. She loved his big goggle eyes and wide smile.

“Let’s stay friends,” she said, and
she kissed his silky green nose.

“Forever?” he croaked.

"Yes, forever!" she croaked back. And they hopped out of the palace and down to the pond, where they lived happily ever after.

Levels for *Read-it!* Readers

***Read-it!* Readers help children practice early reading skills with brightly illustrated stories.**

Red Level: Familiar topics with frequently used words and repeating patterns.

I Am in Charge of Me by Dana Meachen Rau
Let's Share by Dana Meachen Rau

Blue Level: New ideas with a larger vocabulary and a variety of language structures.

At the Beach by Patricia M. Stockland
The Playground Snake by Brian Moses

Yellow Level: Challenging ideas with an expanded vocabulary and a wide variety of sentences.

Flynn Flies High by Hilary Robinson
Marvin, the Blue Pig by Karen Wallace
Moo! by Penny Dolan
Pippin's Big Jump by Hilary Robinson
The Queen's Dragon by Anne Cassidy
Sounds Like Fun by Dana Meachen Rau
Tired of Waiting by Dana Meachen Rau
Whose Birthday Is It? by Sherryl Clark

Green Level: More complex ideas with an extended vocabulary range and expanded language structures.

Clever Cat by Karen Wallace
Flora McQuack by Penny Dolan
Izzie's Idea by Jillian Powell
Naughty Nancy by Anne Cassidy
The Princess and the Frog by Margaret Nash
The Roly-Poly Rice Ball by Penny Dolan
Run! by Sue Ferraby
Sausages! by Anne Adeney
Stickers, Shells, and Snow Globes by Dana Meachen Rau
The Truth About Hansel and Gretel by Karina Law
Willie the Whale by Joy Oades

A complete list of *Read-it!* Readers is available on our Web site: www.picturewindowbooks.com